# The Triumph
# of Death

First staged at the Birmingham Repertory Theatre in March 1981, *The Triumph of Death* presents a mighty panorama stretching from the thirteenth century to the present day. Beginning with the survivors of the mediaeval Children's Crusade, Rudkin's interweaving of history, myth and religion moves on through distorted versions of Joan of Arc, Gilles de Rais and Martin Luther to an acid epilogue in our own times.

'. . . his audiences are rewarded by the finest language to be heard in the theatre today, and glimpses of a drama yet to come from Rudkin, of high wit, passion and lucidity.' (*Times Literary Supplement*)

'. . . he explores the connection between the inner recesses of the personality and social and political forms with a courage that no one else has.' (*Listener*)

*Front cover: a scene from the Birmingham Repertory Theatre production in 1981.*
*Back cover: David Rudkin. Both photographs are reproduced by courtesy of the Birmingham Repertory Theatre.*

*by the same author*

AFORE NIGHT COME (Penguin)
ASHES (Pluto Press)
BURGLARS (Hutchinson)
CRIES FROM CASEMENT AS HIS BONES ARE BROUGHT
    TO DUBLIN (BBC Publications)
THE GRACE OF TODD (Oxford University Press)
HIPPOLYTUS (Heinemann Educational Books)
PENDA'S FEN (Davis-Poynter)
THE SONS OF LIGHT (Eyre Methuen)

David Rudkin

# THE TRIUMPH
# OF DEATH

EYRE METHUEN · LONDON

First published in 1981 by Eyre Methuen Ltd,
11 New Fetter Lane, London EC4P 4EE.
Copyright © 1981 by David Rudkin
ISBN 0 413 49110 2

Printed in Great Britain by Whitstable Litho Ltd, Whitstable, Kent

Set in IBM 10pt Journal by 🗚 Tek-Art, Croydon, Surrey

to

the memory of

Carl Th. Dreyer

# Characters

PAPATRIX, *a monstrous popelike figure*
MOTHER MANUS, *Keeper of his House*
PEEK ⎫
PICKAVANCE ⎬ *scholar-acolytes*
Jesus the Crucified
Stephen of Cloyes, *a mediaeval peasant adolescent*
Three Maimed Survivors of the Children's Crusade, *two boys, one girl*
JEHAN, *crippleback forest-dweller*
GIL ⎫
BRANS ⎬ *her husband-brothers*
VITUS, *her brother*
ULLIN, *his sister-wife*
MOVINS ⎫ *their fathers, drudgery-dulled forest men of*
ABB ⎬ *middle age*
GREISEL, *their mother, dull and fearful*
HENIOT, *the matriarch of all these, now near to death*
PIGLET, *a baby: better a doll properly invested as a baby by the actors*
ENESTER, *young Renascence duke*
ARTAUD, *compassionate fanatic monk*
A BROTHER IN WOOL, *at the Lord's Great Supper*
SISTER AGNES, *at the Supper*
SISTER MARTHA, *at the Supper*
A Junior Judge
A Clerk
An Executioner
Luther

The action of the play takes place ostensibly in the 'middle ages', for this purpose a telescoping of thirteenth fourteenth and fifteenth centuries.

Characters shown here in lower-case are elsewhere manifest or guised in the action as other characters, e.g. Jesus as ENESTER. Some evolve, e.g. Luther from ULLIN. The text makes all such generation plain. The doubling of the Three Maimed Survivors with their descendants JEHAN, GIL and BRANS is obvious. In the Birmingham production the BROTHER IN WOOL doubled as the Clerk and Executioner. Minimum company requirement is as at Birmingham, seven women, eleven men.

*The Triumph of Death* was first presented at the Birmingham Repertory Studio Theatre on 9 March 1981, with the following cast:

| | |
|---|---|
| PAPATRIX | Harold Innocent |
| MOTHER MANUS | Sheila Gish |
| PEEK | Lloyd McGuire |
| PICKAVANCE | Eric Richard |
| STEPHEN  ARTAUD | Steven Crossley |
| THE LORD | Roderic Leigh |
| JEHAN | Veronica Roberts |
| GIL | Jonathan Kent |
| BRANS | Steven Beard |
| VITUS | Terry Molloy |
| ULLIN  MARTIN LUTHER | Mary McCusker |
| MOVINS | Denis Holmes |
| ABB | Nigel Harris |
| GREISEL | Jean Grover |
| HENIOT | Freda Dowie |
| BROTHER IN WOOL | Barkley Johnson |
| SISTER AGNES | Kristin Milward |
| SISTER MARTHA | Jeanette Lewis |

*Directed by* Peter Farago
*Designed by* Christopher Morley
*Lighting by* Brian Harris
*Sound by* Carl Dodds, Jon Mortimer, David Rudkin

The past is another country. The past is not another country.

# Part One

*Within the throbbing vibrance, stroke impending, of a massive
bell. Human whisperings gather like flocks of birds. Gibbering
choral fragments; harsh organ-chords. Bell-vibrance loudening,
painful on the ear. Human babel towering to a shrieking ecstasy
of need: cries of 'Papa! Papa! Pater Sanctus! Pastor nobis!
Father!'. Vast bell-stroke crushes all. From filthy golden gloom,
a dark form, monstrous, slowly materialises to the sight:
PAPATRIX, throned. Face a farded skull of cancerous death.
Crown a Triple Tower, from which diminished human figures
imprisoned scream and reach. Throne (the Hedra) a carved
wooden Gothic city in like idiom — scream, strain and prison
everywhere. Robe a burden of silver, gold. Skeleton hands
bulbous with jewels.*

*In silence PAPATRIX focussing on us. Up through him suddenly
a rectal spasm. His skeleton fingers clasp in anguish a carved
dome, a spire; his skullmouth gasps, fixed in an excretal rictus
like the pit of Hell.*

MOTHER MANUS (*only now we see her*). Our Father speaks.
  (*Her arms tight in, palms up for gifts; her garb a nun-like
  evolution from the Artemis of Ephesus.*)

PAPATRIX (*gasps devour for light and air; his levering skeleton-
  fingers crush carven human mouths and eyes. Rectal parody
  of birth. Suddenly silent, still, hung breathless on the apex
  of his anal travail. Then slow relief.*) Children. Last night the
  Saracen appeared to me again. He stood astride Jerusalem.
  Our Golden Mother, with milk and honey blest! Oh
  children dream with me. The filth in his eyes. The Saracen.
  Above her golden domes and towers, the loathsome parting
  of his creases and his sweating groins. His squat and ordure
  in her golden courts. The lip of his circumcision, hung above
  the Sepulchre of Christ.

*A second fecal spasm; lesser. Ease.*

Children. Pity your Father. My head above you all. Alone,
amid the wind and flame of Heaven. Daily bowed, for all
your sakes, before the awful presence of the Will itself.
Daily, daily to endure for you, burned into me this, that,
another, revelation, of the Will. The Purpose. My long nights
torn for you, how best, how only, through my mediumcy,

that Will Above be given shape on earth; the Purpose there digested and transformed, a plastic ordnance, a code, for you to live by, and be good children.

*Lesser fecal spasms, easing. He slumps in anguish, sweated fingers sliding.*

My daughters and my sons. My free glad children. And how not be glad? Think what we are. Man. Think what is Man. The apex of Creation. The living pattern of the Will in earth. The Saracen bemires your Golden Mother. How are sons and daughters of the Will to live with this? Go. Put this deathly matter to the city and the world.

*A Mass bell tinkles. Two SCHOLARS come, trundle Hedra around, till the side now facing us betokens thick entangling tree. PAPATRIX is gone. MOTHER MANUS, a dark figure, latent. The Scholars — one butch and jovial, PEEK; one lean and austere, PICKAVANCE — lift from beneath the throne the golden pot, steam from its contents rising. In forest shadow they bear the pot with reverence. Now rest awhile.*

PICKAVANCE. Brother Peek.

PEEK. Brother Pickavance.

PICKAVANCE. This utterance we bring. We're men of intellect. Reason. Schooled in Aristotle. Yet here we ride to galvanise the children of a continent to war. There must be some good reason.

PEEK. Cause.

PICKAVANCE. Cause purpose or cause causation?

PEEK. Cause.

PICKAVANCE. No. True reason, in morals, why the Saracen must not continue living. I do, deep in me, feel: the Saracen across the world endangers me. But intuition is no argument.

MOTHER MANUS *beyond there attends the argument; turns to one then the other as he speaks.*

PEEK. Brother Pickavance what is Man? What other creature has sloughed off blind servility to Nature as we have? Hoist himself up from the mud; into language; historical awareness; morality? It must be to some purpose the Will Above endow us so. To further that Will, on earth. The Saracen does not recognise that Will. His very existence in Nature mocks it.

What must the Will do? Transform him, or render him extinct. Nature is slow. She does not have ideas. We are sovereign. We have ideas. It is therefore our responsibility, in Nature, to do her evolutionary work for her; thus implement the Will Above. Exterminate the Saracen.

PICKAVANCE. The Saracen is Man. Of a sort.

PEEK. Appears so. Doubtless so he even thinks himself. Biped, erect, he can't be altogether blamed.

PICKAVANCE. But if he experience himself as Man —

PEEK. Experience? Delusion's an experience.

PICKAVANCE. We experience ourselves as Man.

PEEK. Our experience is authentic. His is not. We have seen God. Uniquely revealed. To us. And in His Image, we, and not the Saracen, are made.

PICKAVANCE. I wish I were so rational as you.

PEEK. Argument is my existence and my joy.

PICKAVANCE. Brother Peek. How are we altogether in God's Image? We are fallible.

PEEK. Ah, but without our freedom to err, there would be no choice. Thus no meaning in our triumph of good.

MOTHER MANUS *approves the argument.*

PICKAVANCE. Forests frighten me. Not without reason the Roman armies dreaded forests. Darker nature. Elf, warlock, wolf . . .

Yes. I see the logic. If we are made in God's Image the Saracen cannot be. And so, and so. But he may argue he is made in his God's image too.

PEEK. Very cunning. An alternative revelation. Contradictory revelations cannot both be true. Two Truths? It is against all mathematics. As well the Sun revolve around two earths.

MOTHER MANUS *is delighted in him.*

PICKAVANCE. What do you say to the problem of death?

PEEK. What is the question?

PICKAVANCE. I see my loved ones. All those, beautiful to me. The ugly too, I must have charity. I cannot believe they die.

PEEK. What does your intuition tell you?

PICKAVANCE. Death has to be a phantom. A grotesque illusion. It seems the end, to us that witness it. But for those who pass, a way to a geography beyond. Where justice, equity prevail; and all accounts that this world got so wrong, are squared. If not, my striving in this life is vain; and my own death to come, a wantonness, already mocking me. I have an obscure conviction, our struggle with the Saracen is somehow to do with this riddle of death.

PEEK. Yes. Your intuition is there before me. I see a connection I had not drawn. A loving God will not blemish His Creation with such a gross excretal act as final death. But the appearance of it: is to a chastening purpose. So too the blemish of the Saracen! He is a phantom too. Oh real, in terms of flesh. Or he would constitute no test of us. How does he test us? His existence is a nagging: that we could — hypothetically but could — be wrong. He lives, and seems a man: where does that leave our special status in Creation? An illusion? All our hope vain, and death shall swallow us? Allow the Saracen any moral credit, you admit the possibility that we are not the unique pattern of the Will. That's the Satanic trick he plays. He is indeed the Devil's construct; and mortal test of our validity. It is the challenge of our time.

*They continue on their way.*

*The Crucified Risen* JESUS *comes before us, in crown of thorns.*

JESUS. Yes. Me. Whom you each make, in your own moral image. How did the war of your children against the Turks begin? In your year twelve hundred and twelve, I am said to have appeared in a vision, to a Stephen of Cloyes, a peasant boy.

*He quietly turns Hedra, third facet to us now: a mediaeval jakes. On it, a rustic thirteenth century adolescent,* STEPHEN. *'Feminine' masculinity, not androgynous but demonic: in him, male and female each inforce the other.*

*Liquid birdsong.*

STEPHEN. Out thou squeeze, brown stinkid sarpint. Lord, the pong of thee. Poor shite, thou'm good for nothin only flies. Flies bain't good till any man. Flies bring us sick-ness. I have a brother for thee. Out thou part. (*Softly whistling, imitating birdsong from outside. Light from* JESUS *the Crucified Risen spreading to illumine him.* STEPHEN *starts up.*) Lord! Jesus! Master — !

JESUS. Hey hey. Hey hey. A shite must not be hurried, take thy time. Who did you say I am?

STEPHEN. Why sir, my Lord. Who suffered and died for me.

JESUS. How is my death a death for thee?

STEPHEN. Why Sir, to take my sin on Thy own back.

JESUS. What is thy sin?

STEPHEN. That I be born Sir. Into sin. Into this world of the flesh and the Devil. Death be our punishment. Unless we love Thee.

JESUS. Do you love me? Stephen? Do you love me? Do you love me?

STEPHEN. I think of Thy agony. To be so full with love for Man, yet find Thyself fallen among Man so ugly and so cruel. The pain Thou must have felt, to burn among us with such love, while us not knowing nailed Thee to the tree.

JESUS. You Stephen? These? (*Nailmarks.*)

STEPHEN (*weeps*). Sir. (JESUS *sits next to him on the jakes.*) Therefore to live we have to love Thee. Thou did conquer Death our punishment.

JESUS. How conquered Death?

STEPHEN. Third day. Thou rosest again.

JESUS. Why?

STEPHEN. To show that Death is not our master. Put Death and Devil in his place.

JESUS. What place is that?

STEPHEN (*ribald*). Thou saidst. Behind us Sir.

JESUS (*amused*). Ah yes. But Stephen. If you love me, how shall that save you from death?

STEPHEN. Not from death, Sir. But from that death into darkness, we hope to be saved. To die not into death but life eternal.

JESUS. Life eternal. What is that?

STEPHEN. Life without end, Sir. In Thy Garden, Sir.

JESUS. Oh Stephen. But in this life. In this body, Stephen's victory over death: what might that be? Love me you say. Love me. How?

JESUS *is vanished.* STEPHEN: *desolation; then stands glorified.*

STEPHEN. A vision. I have had a vision. Lord Jesus spoke with me.

*Comes charging out.* MOTHER MANUS *waits: a nun, severe.*

Lady? Lady? Who are thou? King Jesus spoke with me!

MOTHER MANUS. Jesus lad? What should Our Saviour want to say to thee?

STEPHEN. He — He — (*All clarity of it gone.*) Love him. I must love him. How.

MOTHER MANUS. How indeed. What greater love, than die for him?

STEPHEN. He didn't mean that. I know he didn't.

MOTHER MANUS. How?

STEPHEN. What love for him should dying be? To fall before that conqueror that he himself have slain?

MOTHER MANUS. Very sophisticated. What Jesus says may seem simple. But His words never mean what they seem to mean. His words have to be interpreted boy. Down, down, through all the worlds of less and lesser understanding. Till they make the sense for you that it is right they make.

STEPHEN. He came in the vision to me not you. I understood him while he spoke.

MOTHER MANUS *gently bringing him. Hedra turns its forest side.*

MOTHER MANUS. Stephen. A name for those whom God has chosen. It means a crown. Our Lord's first martyr. Stephen of the stones. István, sainted king of Hungary. You are made for witness, you Stephens of this earth. 'Love him' . . . (*Baring herself: whore naked, plagues and sores; golden hair tumbling.*) I am Jerusalem. Look Stephen where the Saracen's defiled me . . . (*Nesting in the tree above, something of gleaming gold.*) King Jesus calls you for a soldier Stephen. Love Him He says.

He means, Oh Stephen be a golden soldier, make me clean.
(*The gold is armour. A cathedral treble, unearthly pure, soon
heard distant in hymn 'Jerusalem the Golden', tune Ewing,*)
The Saracen has mired me. From all my golden towers, lick
his filth away . . . Head of soldier. Mouth of soldier. Tongue
of golden soldier. Lick me clean . . .

*Darkness covers them. The armour gleams. A children's choir
swells hymn.*

PAPATRIX (*comes, monstrous, haunted*). From Burgundy so
many. Alsace so many. Kolmar, Köln, Ulm . . . France,
twenty thousand. Germany, thirty thousand. Children.
(*Choirs, marchlike.*) To Marseilles . . . Genoa . . . (*Sea-waves
break.*) To march on dryshod to Jerusalem. They said the sea
would part for them. It did not. Two men came to give them
passage. Sent by God. Hugh of Iron, and William the Pig. Off
Sardinia a storm. (*Gale heard yonder; tempestuous sea.*)
Thousands drowned. Those saved, not for Jerusalem at all.
But into Barbary. Sold for slaves. For catamites. For torture,
crucifixion, death of the hooks. Flayed. Impaled. (*Mallets'
quiet systematic tapping. Golden armour hangs: upon a boy
skeleton, anally impaled.*) This was Stephen of Cloyes. You'll
shite no more. The Saracen has stopped you up. Or Arab,
Berber, Riff, all one. Mallet and shaft. Tap tap. Tap tap. Some
long while must this take, and skill. Drive this sharp iron tip
way up in you till out again between your shoulderblades and
yet not puncture any vital organ. Liver, lung, heart. Here's a
guard must live on his post three days. No lad this is not
Jerusalem. Algiers. Tap tap. Tap tap. (*Throbbing vibrance of
the bell. Hell-light, furnace-roar.*) Well, let this be Jerusalem.
And hoist you high toward your heaven as it can.

*Children's singing turning meanwhile to animal screaming.*
MOTHER MANUS, *nun again.*

MOTHER MANUS. Children! Alleluia! And Stephen Alleluia!
You taste death's sting, but pass into a truer life! You meet
King Jesus in His Paradise!

*Smoke begins to cloud the stage.* JESUS *pale beyond, frozen
in an attitude of benediction. Children's hideous screaming;
crackle, spit of burning flesh. Painful vibrance of colossal bell.*
MOTHER MANUS *radiant.*

Children rejoice! You turn to light!

*PAPATRIX huddles on Hedra-foot — city aspect. Pandemonium
fades. Darkness. Windsound distant, waste. Cold statue JESUS
grey. Lingering smoke is mist of night.*

*Three exhausted forms. A lad has lost a leg. Another is blinded.
The girl subject to spasms but seems the power of the three.
Slow make their groping, ruined way.*

*Soon the girl is aware: something from our direction. It
seems smell is her primary sense. Now her sight quickening:
in us, some landmark recognised. She seizes the maimed lad
to show him. He too; unbelieving. Joy. Blind boy, smelling:
he too.*

MAIMED LAD. It is. It is. Home.

BLIND LAD. Home . . .? (*He falls weeping, clutching the earth.*)

GIRL. Now who have a nose? By river and north star. From Holy
Wars, to bring we three tillback again?

*The blind, the maimed, the crazed reach each to us, soldiers
returned. Then suddenly, severally, pause. Scent us anew.*

BLIND LAD. Smell death. Smell death here.

MAIMED LAD. I smell death.

GIRL. Back . . . Into these trees . . .

*They retreat. Are gone.*

JESUS. I too. Retreat from you. (*Withdrawn into darkness.
Gone.*)

*PAPATRIX troubled wakes. MOTHER MANUS, severe.*

PAPATRIX. These dreams.

MOTHER MANUS. Holy Father?

PAPATRIX. The hatred for me in their dying eyes.

MOTHER MANUS. Whose?

PAPATRIX. The tens of thousands. Children. Dying in such
atrocity. Their eyes. Accusing me. 'Our Father sent us here.
Our Father visits this on us.' To die into eternity, severed
from their love of me, oh that's damnation, I have damned
them. From Will Above, through me, to man below, the world
was seamless. I have cracked the world.

MOTHER MANUS. None came home. Their estrangement dies
with them. That's the beauty of war. We must not blame

ourselves. We were wrong. They just as much. They would go. We were in delirium in those days. An age of unreason. Long ago. Now we know better. The Saracen is not a moral problem to us any more. We are rational now.

*Dawn. Thin forest birdsong. What seem subhuman forms crawl wearily up: filthy, brutish, clad in hides — Iron Age men. Waking bleakly into day and drudgery; young, older, men, women; take up in silence their tools of toil: mattock, hoe, two-pronged hoe.*

*Soon from one to another then to others an awareness spreads: some especial scent on the air.*

GIL (*halt, primal*). Sun? Sun light?

MOVINS (*dull, earthbound*). There have been Sun before. Gil brother. Wind still has ice in his beard.

GIL (*young, beneath toil's aging*). Not such sun light as this. Winter have gone. Lent is here. Brothers, sisters, smell her.

BRANS (*young like Gil; seems superficially a 'softer' nature*). A yellow flower open.

*Some hurry to kneel around it.*

GIL. Heniot mother! Heniot mother! Lent have come!

*Some hurry below, soon bring up an old woman HENIOT on a primitive throne of birchwood. She focusses on air and light: but the quickening in her is dark.*

GREISEL (*middle age*). Oh I could dance! (*She doesn't.*) Thank thee, yearth. Thank thee, Sun. Thank, thank, thank.

VITUS (*young, morally apart*). Thank thank. Winter shall still end. We could all on us be dead in its black night, still should this lent be come.

HENIOT. Well Vitus: lent have come. And we are living. Bring me my husbands.

*Two skulls, long fixed, totemlike, to walking-poles. These she stakes firmly either side of her, hand grimly grasping each.*

BRANS (*hurrying with something preciously covered in a hide*). Mother! Look what I have made the Sun!

*She opens it; all watch attentive, as children a marvel. A clumsy birchwood bowl.*

A bowl. To gladden him.

VITUS. For Sun to eat from, brother Brans?

BRANS. No Vitus brother. To put in water.

VITUS. For Sun to drink from? Have Sun a mouth?

BRANS. For when he be high above us in the sky. In this water see his light glint back at him. (*He puts water into the bowl.*) Heniot mother. I have thought this gift in my head through the dark winter. And made it while you rest were sleeping. For if he come again. Mother. Do you say this be a good thanks?

HENIOT. I do. Aymen. I do.

BRANS (*places the bowl on a stump in mid-clearing*). Sun. This I make thee. For to stand in middle of this world, for thy great gladness; and our thanks, that thou be strong again, and come to us with lent and summer.

OTHERS. Aymen. Aymen.

VITUS. I hope no cloud come.

JEHAN (*seems to be with* GIL; *early pregnant; also some awkwardness in the spine*). Cloud rain or storm, the gift is given.

*She touches* BRANS' *face in affection: seems to be 'with' him too. Indeed, the three of them.*

HENIOT. Vitus?

VITUS. He rise he set. How, I don't know. He rise he set, spite of all us. Lent follow winter, spite of us.

ULLIN (*with* VITUS; *in papoose on her back a child*). We must work.

*They move away. Alone of them the pregnant girl does not take up a heavy implement. She feels shame.*

HENIOT. Yehan. Daughter.

JEHAN (*bitter at inadequacy, bringing a hide bundle from below*). Yehan's work. To chit these setts. (*She kneels opening the bundle, to spread small dark potato-seed.* [Yes.])

*She begins a careful rubbing, here, there on each, removing all chits but two; apart from white stragglers the chits need not be visible to us. On a larger sett, she'll leave four chits, two each end.*

Cripple work. My crooked back.

HENIOT. That too must be done. (*Of the skulls:*) He were cripple. He were blind. Atween us three we got this folk begun.

JEHAN. Haha. Blind father's eyes let the light in now. Oneleg father, leg he did have, same loss till him now. Yet my poor back. I wish the Lord might make it whole.

HENIOT. Why? You being born so.

JEHAN. For I see I may take but a weak share in we'r toil for ever. My life to come, a cripple path. If life we shall have, after you die.

HENIOT. I die soon.

JEHAN. Us know.

HENIOT. You live after. I shall be shrunk till these, then dust, then nothing. Lent shall still come. The light shall not go out with me. I did not bring it.

JEHAN. Mother, thou brought it. In beginningless dark, thou were first to spring till light. You tell us.

HENIOT. You shall live after. That I tell thee.

JEHAN. More then wish I this healed. (*She pauses to stretch her spine, alleviating sacrum.*) For sake of this birth. I dread. Mother. Afore thou die. Speak to the Lord.

HENIOT. Him? Master? Think I mun only say Master and *He* come?

JEHAN. He shall call us soon. Now lent have come. Till His Great Supper. For Bread and Wine and Fellowship in Him. Heniot mother, ask Him then. His healing touch on Jehan's poor back.

HENIOT. Why I ask?

JEHAN. Thou are His sister!

HENIOT. He'm Lord of earth and sky, how am I His sister?

JEHAN. Thou were first He made. From blind dull clay to gladden Him, alone on His dark yearth.

HENIOT. Ay so I've told thee. Glad him, ha? Why should He make me husbands then?

JEHAN. For thou to get by; and us folk begin.

HENIOT. Who do you say He is, this Lord?

JEHAN. Why, Master of the earth. Lord of All Tenderness.

HENIOT. And you love Him.

JEHAN. Mother.

HENIOT. And you love Him.

JEHAN. Fast I do.

HENIOT. You love him.

JEHAN. He is our life. I have only to stop in my poor work, I think of Him. My love for Him leap in my heart.

HENIOT. More than for your husbandbrothers Gil and Brans?

JEHAN. In His love I love them. When we'm twined in the dark I feel His arms around us all. While we sleep, I know He watches us.

HENIOT. Speak to the trees. Lent have come. Lord wakes. He'll be about the world. The trees might whisper of thy need.

JEHAN. Oh mother. Thou talk daft.

HENIOT. Speak to the trees. In the telling you might learn better what you need.

JEHAN *works on. Warmer.* HENIOT *dozes.* JEHAN *listens. Strange forest sounds. Hum of spring. Sudden woe of her spine. A decision. Soundless, not to waken* HENIOT, *she puts her work down, steals a little way aside. She plays her game amid the trees: eyes shut, ears tilted for the sough above, fingers searching the bark for its identifying pattern.*

JEHAN Beechtop (*this she hears would be a full rustling*). Aspen (*a dry thin rustling*). Birk bark (*mocking shriek of green woodpecker started up above*). Yaffle. Mock thy yaffling. (*Sends own mocking yaffle after.*) Oh if I could fly . . . (*Whispering into the tree:*) Birk wood. Listen till Jehan what she ask. Some help for her poor back. Whisper in Master's ear: Some help for Jehan's back. If pipe be cut from thee, let thy tune be: Master, Master. There be a wrongness in poor Jehan's bone, badshapen. Only the Lord Himself could set that true. A touch of Thy Healing, Lord, on my poor back . . .

*He is already here: a white figure, ragged, mortal. He was* JESUS *before; she knows him as* THE LORD.

THE LORD. Master you call me. Lord you say. Look at me.
(*Still* JEHAN *dare not.*) Do you love me?

JEHAN. Master.

THE LORD. Jehan do you love me?

JEHAN. Master. Sir . . .

THE LORD. Do you love me?

JEHAN. Master, Thou are Lord of all our love.

THE LORD. Look at me.

> JEHAN *turns. Sees. Astonished.*

Not in the shape you thought to see. By day I go in likeness
of a man.

JEHAN. My love! Oh J —

THE LORD. Never my name! Jehan. Never my name. Once only,
in their last agony for me, my lovers may call me by my name.
To tell the world . . . the King of Love is fallen from His
Heaven.

JEHAN. A— gon— y . . . ? Thou use dark words with me. What
is a-gon-y?

> HENIOT *is here.*

THE LORD (*simple*). Mother Heniot.

HENIOT (*simple*). Master.

> JEHAN *amazed. They sit.*

HENIOT. Jehan daughter. What do you say is the world?

JEHAN. Why mother. This. . . These trees . . .

HENIOT. What be beyond these?

JEHAN. Mother! What can be beyond the world? There's why
thou have never let us wander from each other's hearing.
Fear we might come sudden on the end of this world and
stumble off.

HENIOT. Thou have wandered today.

THE LORD. Jehan. Where do you say is the middle of this
world?

JEHAN. Sir? In our garden we have made. (THE LORD *waits.*)
The stump of a tree. Where my husbandbrother Brans have

this day set his bowl with water in to glad the Sun. That
stump of a tree is the birthstring of the earth.

THE LORD. Are you the only in this world?

JEHAN. There do be others. That do come together with us till
Thy Supperside.

THE LORD. Where do these others dwell?

JEHAN. We do only see they at the Suppers.

THE LORD. Between the one great Supper and the next, where
do you say they dwell?

JEHAN. I do have never asked me. Thou call, they come.

THE LORD. Ask now. See in your head. What if these others also
have a garden in this world? Stripped of trees by their own
drudgery? Their ground they break for tilling too? Cattle with
them too? Sheep, swine. A charcoalbury for to smelt their
iron too?

JEHAN. I do never have thought.

THE LORD. Think now. How they others too might have among
them one, a Brans but with another name, make also him some
gift to the Sun? Set that on their stump of a tree their mother
tell them is the birthstring of the earth?

JEHAN. Thou trouble me.

THE LORD. Be troubled more. What if, as your garden be amid
this world, so all this world of trees lie in a greater garden yet.
Beyond, and round about this all, a greater world you never
thought could even be.

JEHAN. Thou tell me this to frighten me.

THE LORD. Mother Heniot. Take her. (*Blindfolding her.*) Show
her. And rest be on you both. (*Gone.*)

HENIOT (*heart heavy*). I die soon. One among you must put
child behind him.

JEHAN. Mother?

HENIOT (*stepping first one skullpole forward then the other
then herself,* JEHAN *clinging to her*). We three shall lead
thee. In this at least we've no great hurry. Not before twilight
dare we come. Till the edge of the world. (*Gone.*)

*Hot.* GIL *toiling, pauses. Looks up at the Sun. Kneels, face to the sky.*

GIL. Thank thee, Sun. Great Sun, that thou be well again, and strong, I thank thee. Safe day across thy sky Sir. And no cloud harm thee.

VITUS (*has seen*). 'Thank the Sun'!

GIL. To thank in truth. Sun has no ears, I know that. But to be glad in my heart, this lent be come. And raise that gladness high.

VITUS. Delve, mattock, dib, rake, scrat: Lent means us breaking up this ground her third time. Gladness?

BRANS. Look. A ant. Carry this great splinter.

*All gather.*

There.

*They crouch, watch like children,* VITUS *no less so.*

MOVINS. Think a man. Carry a tree on his back such a size.

BRANS. Clever ant. Strong.

VITUS. Slips though. Up over this little ridge of dust. Can't make it. Gil. Keep slipping back, look. Try. Try.

MOVINS. A man. Carry a tree. Up a slope such steepness.

GREISEL. Oh. Slip again.

BRANS. Gil what you doing?

GIL. Help him. Reach the top . . .

BRANS. How can you help a ant?

GIL. I do have higher sight. Easy . . . Easy . . .

*Suddenly:*

OTHERS (*disappointed*). Oh. (*Silence.*)

BRANS. Never do that. Never do that. Cast on his back, his legs a-wavin in the air, he'm helped now good and true. Where's that splinter now, was worth such drudgery till him? Lost it. Lost. Help him see it can you, wi' your higher sight? Your high hand rest it on his back for him again? 'Help him': fallen from his path, as he was not before? His burden lost and all his toil undone? Fool brother.

GIL (*astonished*). Thank you. Brans. Brother. You do set me true. I was wrong. Ant. I am sorry. I did you wrong.

ULLIN. We must work now. Ground be broken up its third time for the seed.

*They go.*

HENIOT *brings* JEHAN *before us. Takes the blindfold off her.* JEHAN *sees, and turns from us appalled.*

HENIOT. Think no more Mother Heniot were beginning of the world. Think no more with Mother Heniot Sun sprang to light or night sky all a sudden pricked wi stars. Think no more Lord moulded me from clay to gladden Him, alone in His dark earth. I come from flesh. From out that world. Flesh there, folk, many, so many and so many, thou shall never tell their number. I had a mother and a father. So had this man. So had he. Their mothers, fathers, mothers' mothers, fathers' fathers, flesh, flesh, back, back, beyond them ever, in that world.

JEHAN: *a desolate wailing cry, her Eden rent.*

Sad, lass? Knowledge. And keep it to thyself. Jehan only I awake. Open your eyes. Look at this world. What folk be in it? They have a Lord. Of Love. Nailed living to a tree. Hands, feet. And he so struggles to be free. Day, night and day they hammer in the nails again. For this, they call themselves good Crosstian folk. I call them vampires. I call them the undead. They fatten on each others' blood. They have no backholes, and they cast no shadow. They live by something they call money, which is the shit of toil. The name of their true Master is the Devil. Lord of Death.

Well. There's a world, and here's a world. Hold both in your head. You must. And when I die, keep you your brother-sisters warm, and safe, as I have done; and tell them nothing. Our Lord's our Master still.

Weep. Brans' gift to the Sun was set this morning on the birthstump of the earth. Now that's the centre of the world no more.

*Rain's dull pelt. Damp smoulderglow, weary groups huddling:* MOVINS *with* GREISEL *and* ABB; ULLIN *with* VITUS *nursing and joggling floppyheaded baby;* GIL *with* BRANS.

VITUS (*zooming his nose into the baby and out again*). Little pig I love thee. Little pig I love thee. Oh thou do look funny. Piglet lad, thou do look funny. Poop!

ULLIN. We mun have Mother Heniot give piglet a name.

VITUS. Who'm afeared on the big bad wolf? Whooooh! Howwwwwh!

ULLIN. Vitus! You'll start them.

*Silence: all listen, peopling surrounding dark with wolves.*

GREISEL. They'm lost. Mother and Jehan.

BRANS. How can Mother be lost in the world?

*He is quietly scraping at a small wooden instrument through which he every so often blows a soft imperfect note.*

I reckon she mun say farewell to every tree afore she die.

ULLIN. She mun make piglet his name afore she die.

GREISEL. Well where do Jehan be to?

GIL. With her. She must show someone where the greenworts grow, afore she die.

GREISEL (*ponders this*). Why Jehan?

VITUS. Jehan can't carry nothin' heavier Ma Greisel, that'm for why.

GREISEL. In this rain? Mother of all things, she should know when night shall come.

ABB. Rain caught her.

GREISEL. Wolf caught her.

MOVINS. Wander too far, stumble on edge of world and tumble off.

BRANS. Heniot mother? Fall off her own making?

GIL. World must end somewhere. For Sun to pass below and up again. He'm under us now. (*He dunts the ground with his heel.*)

ULLIN (*nursing*). It be some wonder.

VITUS. Ullin?

ULLIN. And you reckon. They other folks at the Lord's Great Supper. How mother Heniot can be their mother too.

BRANS. Ullin, how not?

ULLIN. How many they be. Don't seem to have tore her about so bad. And they don't dwell with us. Reckon though to farry a bab in this world we mun find some better way. (*Pause; baby feeding.*)

GIL. Shall be soon now.

MOVINS (*head dozing*). What?

GIL. When Lord shall call us to the Supper.

BRANS (*deep gladness*). Yes. When Lord shall thrust his great cock up me.

GIL. Bain't I enough?

BRANS. He be the Lord.

ABB. Hush that.

GIL. Dad.

BRANS. Dad.

GREISEL. Mother Heniot die, might be no Supper.

*Silence.*

MOVINS. We should sleep. Spuds to set tomorrow. Winter wet, this lent wind cold, now rain again: make yearth like stone to work.

JEHAN *comes shuddering, with armful of drash and smaller branches.*

BRANS. Where you bin then? Gathering wood? Thou? Wood? Lose thy path?

JEHAN. No.

GIL. Thou, but. Jehan. Wood.

JEHAN. Not heavy. Drash. To start our fires. Must help you! (*She kneels there, contemplating her two men. Some joy she knows this earth can never give her now.*)

*On Hedra* PAPATRIX. *No crown now. Hair long, putrescent as after disinterment. Light has quality of methane gas.* PEEK, PICKAVANCE *stand grave; a third similar figure beyond, obscure.*

PAPATRIX. There is a blemish in the earth. I went a night-journey above the multitudes of Man. Their faces were upturned to me, in loving song. Father! Father! I stooped to them that mouth of mine. As though I were the moon, I drew the heaving swell of them behind me there across the turning globe, each one man straining not to be lost, reaching to vouchsafe in the tickle of his little tongue his gladness in me, oneness with me; authenticating me.

I came to pass above a silent forest. Silent of men. Silent of their song. Was I mistaken? This not forest, but the sea? I gazed behind me, down. The texture of it eddied, cross-currented, disturbed: green, dark, unquiet in the night. Forest. Men in it. And I above them and they did not know it. I stooped, down, down, those lips of mine, quartering that forest, quartering it all. No answer. Some defect in their making, and could not sense me. Men; and have no Father in their dreams? Lost children. Tears for them sprang in my eyes. Dread for them. Shuddering I rose, my head into Heaven, and all this dark globe below came lifting into sight, rim to far curved rim of it. All that earth, had been so living in its song for me, was shrunken, cold dead crust of stone, and fissuring with cracks.

*He pauses. He can see this still.* PEEK, PICKAVANCE *listen in terror.*

Wherefore. In this light of day and reason. We must enquire. What blemish in the earth might send such intimation to me in the night. Whose forest? Where? And what lost Man these ignorant children are. Bring me the world.

*The third figure comes, with open heavy mediaeval tome, a Register of Man. A scholar-monk, maturer than the other two:* ARTAUD, *reincarnation of* STEPHEN, *fanatically close-shaven, his erotic intensity a ravening love for the One True Truth of things. Gentle; sad for all lost sons and daughters.*

ARTAUD. We think we know already. (*He shows.*)

PAPATRIX. Him? Our severest pillar of the north? In his estate? Lord Enester?

ARTAUD. He.

PAPATRIX. He must be ignorant of it.

ARTAUD. More then his responsibility.

PICKAVANCE (*apart*). I am puzzled by Our Father's usage. He speaks of Earth, he speaks of World. I think I see the distinction he draws —

PEEK. Earth is Nature. The elemental datum. World is order, institution, Man.

PICKAVANCE. He says a blemish in the earth. Id est, that these lost children in the forest are a defect in Creation.

PEEK. A residuum of Nature, awaiting integration with the Will.

PICKAVANCE. I am troubled. Suppose though, that in their nature too —

ARTAUD. It is in a sheep's nature to stray. The sheep is no less lost. Who respected a sheep's nature, what shepherd would he be?

*He stamps, as a soldier to smarten the hang of his uniform; clasps a military belt around his habit.* PEEK, PICKAVANCE *likewise, depart.* MOTHER MANUS *comes; as last seen.*

MOTHER MANUS. What guise was best, to penetrate Duke Enester's castle? Where men are strongest, there they fall. I am Death. Most are more than half in love with me already. None can resist my advances. Not in the grave my proper parish. But in this life. Wedlock? There's a kingdom of the dead. My most successful exploitation of a natural resource. Earth's racing mire of sexuality, churning harnessed to the business of the world. Yet I could marry this Bluebeard if he be; as mere wife, still his seventh door be locked to me. While love. Desire. That turns a man to flame and burns all world from him . . . More so, forbidden love. Make him an exile in this world; and I alone, home country to his heart. In my forbidden arms, stroke all his private being bare. (*Beneath the habit we see she is in a young man's tunic; she changes sex before our eyes.*) I shall surprise his heart. Burn him alive. Cold heart, his, I hear; numb from some pain. Cold, numb, it's still his heart, and can be pierced still. No great step from pierce to break a heart; then that last aching of it into stone. (*Puts in contact lenses, irises jet black.*) World, Devil, Death, I'm on my way to Him.

*Storm. Night.* ENESTER *with lantern; to* ARTAUD, *soldier now with warrant.*

ENESTER. Shelter?

ARTAUD. Sir. (*He has assumed a rural accent.*) Only till morning Sir. Or this storm pass. A stable Sir . . .

ENESTER. Men in stable straw . . . Stench and mire . . .

*Surely this the Lord whom* JEHAN *saw.*

ARTAUD. A stenchy business Sir, a-keepin the State clean.

ENESTER. But a stable. Duke Enester no room in his house for the unknown traveller by night? Captain, who's to know he be not talking to the Lord?

ARTAUD. Who indeed Sir.

ENESTER. Come in to the fire. Bring your men. How many?

ARTAUD. Myself and two Sir. Three. Sir? Also one other. He would contaminate your house. If he he can be called. A prisoner on his way to burning.

ENESTER. I heard of no trial.

ARTAUD. Trial, then burning. Sir. Young man. Witchcraft. Heresy . . .

ENESTER. ?

ARTAUD. And the — abominable crime. With this last charge he'm hardly likely to be Jesus is he?

ENESTER. I am sure he is not. Stable there for him. Kitchen for you soldiers.

*Soldiers* PEEK *and* PICKAVANCE *trundle witchcart on, in which an obscure figure, in posture of maltreatment.*

ENESTER (*peers at the warrant*). Mortalis.

ARTAUD. Moralis Sir.

ENESTER. A sorrow for him, he were not moral as his name. To burn Thursday. Witchcraft and heresy. Is it true? These kiss the Prince of Darkness in his sty parts? True, their broomstick is a phallus-head concealed with twigs? True, up in these, their Master's spunk comes cold?

PEEK. Ask him yourself Sir. Let him shite through his own mouth, not sully ours.

ENESTER. No. Never sully yours. In, a moment. For this, my hospitality of hoof and mire. Who's kissed the Devil's dungvalve should find my stable stench a eucharist. I've ripe horses. He's manacled?

PEEK. The ankles be smashed Sir. Saves chains. (*A mallet swings from his belt.*)

*They go.* ENESTER *approaches the cart.*

ENESTER. Witchcraft and heresy. They make you a man of parts. Moralis. For your last end. Fine carriage to ride, who once was ridden.

MOTHER MANUS *stirs, 'MORALIS' there.*

MORALIS (*rural speech also*). They break my ankles, have to carry me. Price they pay.

ENESTER. This, for burning? Oh here shall be some spit and crackle Thursday. Male breast shrivel, roasted arm drop sheer off. A manhood, burn? Miregate, postern: burn? Oh that's morality. If I were a married man, my children would bring chestnuts Thursday afternoon, to roast at your feet.

MORALIS. Not married, Master?

ENESTER. But I shall.

MORALIS. Why?

ENESTER. Only in wifebed is our Adam hallowed. For progeny.

MORALIS. Clumsy Creator God. To mismake fathering a spasm and sneeze good moral man must hallow? One man one wife in one obedient narrow bed, for brood alone?

ENESTER. Rail against matrimony. It is holy. You wed Thursday. Your husband is the stake. The blessed Augustinus says . . .

MORALIS. What?

ENESTER. . . To burn Thursday . . . Having such . . . dark eyes . . .

MORALIS. Mine will be dark. Seeing where they have seen. They hold the image of their Master in them. Look. See his face.

ENESTER. Dreams . . . Dreams . . .

MORALIS. What's a dream? I dream I fly. I wake in bed. Limbs aching. The witches rode me in my sleep, to Meon Hill. I say I wake hagridden. You dream by day. Burning me, you dream you purge the earth of me. But your stake brings us into being. You need us: for that dark, by which your light seems light. Who the dreamer, which the dreamed?

ENESTER. Poor broken feet. This, to burn? How could I burn this? No . . . No . . .

MORALIS. What are you saying Enester?

ENESTER. These could be healed . . .

MORALIS. For me to stand when I burn?

ENESTER. I know a greenwife in the forest . . .

MORALIS. Forest Sir? Green woman?

ENESTER *is about to answer; he sees:*

ARTAUD (*returned with* PEEK, PICKAVANCE *to trundle* MORALIS *away to the stable*). Learn all you want Sir?

ENESTER. Oh. I am astonished.

(*Alone.*) And my own sex? Always assumed, only poor sick others fell that way. Enester?

I was always too much head. Too much the ferryman for others to their dreams. For once do first, think after. Ferryman for once myself ride my dark water.

*High sunlight. Rooks' wheeling, disturbed afar.* JEHAN *comes anxiously, rake in hand: to* VITUS.

JEHAN. Vitus?

VITUS. She would walk. All round. At each tree listen. Touch its bark. 'Aspen' she'd say: 'far well. Beech, far well. Oak . . . Larch . . .' She watched you all a while. Your work. Then she knelt by the stump. She looked up toward the Sun. 'Thank you for my life. Far well.' She laid her down. 'Have Jehan come. Then all you others. To bring me till our Holy Ground.'

*A moment. Then* JEHAN *off his way, he hers.*

*Rooks nearer.* ENESTER *cautiously comes, bowed with* MORALIS *on his shoulders. He gently lays him down.*

ENESTER. You are my second Cross. Gladly I bear you. Today's Green Thursday, and you should have burned. Tomorrow's Bad Friday, but I rise already. . . This is their holy ground.

MORALIS. Where is this wise woman you say shall set me right? How shall you present me to her tribe? So innocent you describe them, they have no place for me in their theology.

ENESTER. Our Great Lent Supper falls tonight. You know the Calendar. Why, you come timely.

MORALIS. You wcre ripe. What shall you tell them I am?

ENESTER. 'Brothers. Sisters. One I love. Guard him, safe, my joy, in this green forest from the sick world's wolf and flame . . .' Oh my dark angel . . .

MORALIS. How dark?

ENESTER. Dark, so fair. Fair to me, so dark.

*He would kiss* MORALIS' *ankles;* MORALIS *withdraws them as in pain.*

MORALIS. And you will marry.

ENESTER. For dynasty.

MORALIS. Alas poor Bluebeard.

ENESTER. I never remember your face. When I am from you, I try to picture you. Always this that another feature of you swims from my fixing. I see you now. Why, so you are. How could you not be printed on my memory? I look away, and you dissolve again. Except these eyes. Where was Enester before I saw these eyes? When I saw these first, no inkling what they were to do to me.

MORALIS. Find me this sister.

ENESTER. Not yet. Not yet. You'll be among these long enough. Strange. We've left their hand-drawn plough so far behind. Yet is our farmer's day less wearisome and long? For all we rise, we bring our toil up with us. New tools new drudgery. Some umbilicus to the grindstone. Original Sin. The Devil in us, disquieted at play.

MORALIS. Why are you afraid of silence?

ENESTER. For fear you speak. And tell me that you find me ugly.

MORALIS. When I stand again, I promise you I'll bring you down into my bed.

ENESTER. You are not Moralis. That is your dayname only. You are not moral in the night. What is your name of night? by which your chosen call you?

MORALIS. You'll learn it when I come with you.

ENESTER. My dark lady. You man me, woman me, unman me. I was born under Cancer indeed. Brittle shell, so easy pierced; within, soft quick, and water of the sea — (*To kiss him —* )

JEHAN *coming.* ENESTER *makes toward her* — GIL, BRANS, VITUS, MOVINS, ABB, ULLIN, GREISEL *come; some with poles from which skulls have half-decomposed, others clumsily carrying a blood-and-shit-stained pallet on which the shrunken cancerous husk of* HENIOT *lies, half-curled onto her side, every jolt, movement, twist, an agony almost to extinction of her.*

HENIOT. This is my last path . . . Belly all afire . . . Innards boiled till black water . . . Oh — (*Spasm of retching.*) My mouth's a arsehole now . . . Leave me down.

ULLIN. Oh. Mothermother, afore thou die, piglet his name.

HENIOT. Abb. Son. Movins. Son. Greisel. Daughter. See you burn my body. Burn it all.

ULLIN. Mam, bab his name. Mother! Can't leave little piglet in this world without no name.

ABB. Name, no name: for bab all one. Sky shall go black on us now. (*He buries his head in the ground, a suffocated wailing.*)

HENIOT. Fool, Abb. I tell thee.

ULLIN. Mother, a name for our son!

HENIOT. Jehan. Keep these safe. (*Seizing her.*) Here's a world. Hold both together. Lord's your Master still. Burn me all. For fear I haunt ye.

Husband? Husband? Wind took your heads away. Lay beside me. This sweet grass. (*Or 'This sweet earth' if stage-floor has a peaten surface.*)

Her'm hereabout. Filthy black sow.

*Almost a shaking of the fist. All look where* HENIOT *seems to see Death coming: as from us. Instinctively they part to leave Her path.*)

Oh . . . Oh . . . (*Surprise:*) This?

*She is gone. Silence.* ABB, GREISEL, MOVINS *have buried their heads, flinching from sky's fall.*

*Nobody dare move.*

*Forest sounds filter in again; soon the baby's crying, off.* GIL, BRANS, VITUS, ULLIN; *each cheats himself into seeing again, what this new Heniotless world may be.* JEHAN *must show nothing of what she knows.*

VITUS. Movins. Abb. Father. Father. Greisel-mother. Sun still shine. Mother farewell.

GIL. Mother, farewell. (BRANS *can only gape at* HENIOT's *deadness.*) Movins. Abb. Say mother farewell.

MOVINS. Mother?

ABB. Lady Mother?

*He and* MOVINS *squat gazing at her, blinking, dull.*

ULLIN (*at last*). What do we do now?

GIL *and* VITUS *think.*

GIL. Burn her.

VITUS. Off her head first, I get the axe.

GIL. No Vitus, head and all. She say. Burn her all.

VITUS (*thinks*). Then husbands too.

GREISEL (*leaps forward, clasping poles*). No! Father! Father!

GIL. Greisel they be only poles.

MOVINS. Burn they, we'm alone!

VITUS. We are alone.

GIL. Head, husbands, pallet, all. Chair too.

GREISEL *screams.*

VITUS. Greisel! Movins, Abb! Help carry your mother. Jehan, that kindling she set thee carrying, now we see why. Ullin, feed that piglet.

GIL. Vitus, wrong. You lean your will upon us all. 'Carry, feed, fetch, carry'. You hurl your will on others, Vitus. Wrong.

VITUS. What do Gil say do? Leave these weep?

BRANS. We should weep.

GIL. I don't know . . .

BRANS. If only we could ask the Lord.

ULLIN. Brans say true, we must ask the Lord.

VITUS. Ullin, wife, the Lord's not here. We are here. And feed that piglet.

BRANS. The Lord is here. We may not see him, in His loveliness by day: but He is here. He watches us.

VITUS. Ask him then.

BRANS *is silent.*

JEHAN. I say burn her, then work. We've not the time to weep.

VITUS. Jehan bring that wood. (*All bear* HENIOT *on the pallet away, discovering that her 'husbands' can be used as shafts.*)

ENESTER *emerges.*

ENESTER. Moralis. Friend. Too late to bring the greenwife to you now. But the daughter . . . Moralis? Moralis? . . ? Who could not walk . . .? Angel? Hex me . . .? To wake my heart then flay it raw? Oh heart . . . (*He falls to his knees.*) Whence this mist before the Sun . . .? Smoke . . . Sweet pork of human burning . . . Moralis? Oh where is my Dark Lady, where is he?

Eyes clear. Heart cold. The Calendar calls. Moon full tonight, Pan wake. Bring joy to the world. Priest, summon others to their dreams.

*Covert, dark: softly whistles a summoning Naturlaut: swift up an octave, down a sharpened fourth. Again.*

The night that I was born, the fishermen cried out, Great Pan is dead! From the cliffs of Crete and crags of Syria: Pan ho Mégas téthnikè!

*Again that summons, more incisive, twice.*

I wake. I walk. Tonight's our Supper. Bretheren, sisters, bring your cakes and wine. (*He hurries away.*)

*Afternoon light. Heniot's clan heavyhearted, work.* ULLIN *has her baby in the papoose. Here one with a mattock breaking heavy earth, here another with a hoe, here another with a rake drawing a fine tilth, another with heavy stone smashing clods to dust;* VITUS *not working, simply watching them.*

GIL. Vitus? Brother? Friend in living? Thou be sad? Work's best when sad.

VITUS. Ay. I see you.

GIL. Vitus brother, thou be sick?

VITUS. How sick? Not be working, that make sick of me?

GIL. Vitus?

VITUS. I'll not work.

GIL. Vitus thou must.

VITUS. How must?

GIL. Not work not eat.

VITUS. What make that so?

GIL. It be so. Brother.

VITUS. I may take my food from what you grow.

GIL. Vitus brother, thou may not.

VITUS. Not may, but can. Eat these beans, come summer. Your
work have planted. What's to let me?

ULLIN. Vitus . . .?

*The others watch in bleak herdlike stupor.*

VITUS. I shall not work, yet eat these beans. I say this. No sky
fall on me. There is no sky. Make me work.

ULLIN. Vitus . . .

*In GIL a new sensation: frustration, wrath. Spade raised, with
a lunging animal roar he is suddenly doing something new to
their experience: hurling himself against a friend in violence.
The moment of Cain is on him. But GIL cannot carry the
stroke through. The arm that had raised it seems to him
possessed; the hand is something of its own. In misery he
makes to chop it off. BRANS, JEHAN, ULLIN cry out,
prevent him.*

ULLIN. Fool Gil. No hand no work. Oh Gil . . . Oh Vitus . . .

VITUS. There who went to lean his will upon a man?

GIL. Not work, yet live from our work: you lean your will upon
us all.

VITUS. How shall you make me work then?

*Silence.*

GIL. A cloud is covering the Sun.

*Afar, the whistling summons. Each has heard, all severally
pause. Again, sharp, clearer, a little nearer. Through them all
a deep change coming: joy. They gather implements, hurry
away.*

*Stillness. Sunset light. One blackbird's liquid evening song; pebbly rattle of stonechat.* ENESTER. *Sober, in full moral evaluation of all he does, discarding Renascence splendour to thin white nakedness, item by item dons instead: rank black hairy fleece, sleeves, breeches. He pauses, listens: stonechat alone; a solitary crow heard croak its dark flight away; twilight. Now* ENESTER *is donning: cloven buskins of horn, rank gloves of cloven horn; an artificial phallus, a little broader and longer than average human size, testicles pendant like a bull's — a desultory squeeze, fine jet of water. Now the headpiece, goat with splendid crown of horns. Factual before us, paradoxically the Immanence Itself. HIM, present: Satan, Cernunnos, Pan, call Him what you will. Night. In his hoofhand a syrinx-reed. From this He sends out now his summons: pure rising octave, angular falling sharpened fourth — eldritch, unquieting. Again. He is listening. Soon, from behind us, distant answering, a tone higher to enhance the sense of distance: similar, but rawer, cruder.* ENESTER PANICUS *turns from us northward. Thither the same summons, thence soon a similar clumsier pipe replies.* PAN *sends his summons eastward now, and west. All around us gathering, a multiplicity of answers, tritonous and harsh.*

*Deep night. On the brink of our subsonic threshold a tremor begins; and the crack, crackle of mould, bast. thicket, brake, a very waking of the earth. A mist the white of milk is rising; and behind the Horned God waiting like a priest, the blank nectarine disc of the moon begins to mount the sky. A ceremonial human droning: from behind us, beside us, among us, all sides yonder. Man, woman, young, child, old, in workday hides, others in garments of wool, others in white, from all around to Him there gathering:*

> — I was glad when Thou called to me,
>   Arise and come until Thy Dwelling, Lord . . .
> — Lord, Thou call, I come to Thee . . .
> — I was at work and heard Thee: Lord, I
>   come to Thee . . .
> — Lord of my soul, Who make me live, I
>   hear Thee and I come to Thee . . .
> — Lord I seek Thee, hear my cry . . .
> — My soul doth raise Thee Lord so high,
>   Thou are so dear to me . . .

*What follows is simple, informal, not ritual at all.* PAN's *voice genuinely gently rusticised:*

PAN. Friends in living, let us greet each other.

*They do so, kissing each other: 'Brother,' 'Sister . . .'*

PAN (*informally, to one then other:*) Brother . . . Sister . . .

MOVINS. An heavy news to tell you, Lord. Goodmother Heniot is dead.

ABB. Our mother Sir.

PAN. My sister. Yes.

*They are settling into a circle, Him at the head, unwrapping cakes and wine. One clay drinking-grail. Never does this become iconic: it could almost be a picnic of the Women's Institute.*

We should give thanks for our sister's life.

*They do so, each in his or her own silence.*

SISTER AGNES (*in white*). Master? Does she worship with us? Does she sit among us at this Supper, only we cannot see?

PAN. I think we must say that she does not. Sister Agnes. We must take it fully into us that she is dead. She is not anywhere at all.

A BROTHER IN WOOL. Lord it is easy for Thee. Thou are the earth. Thou do not die.

*PAN says nothing.*

ULLIN (*nudging VITUS*). Ask Him. Ask Him.

VITUS. Thou ask Him.

ULLIN. Thou ask Him Vitus. Thou'm the man.

PAN. Sister Ullin? Ask me what?

ULLIN. That Thou shine Thy face upon our little piglet. Shed blessing on our son.

VITUS. Ay Lord.

*PAN takes the baby in his rank arms.*

ULLIN. And Thou say it be a good name, Sir, we would call him Vitusson.

PAN. You bore him. You carried him.

ULLIN. He be the father.

PAN. If you will. Vitusson, I make on your head the ancient

sign of brotherhood. (*What we have taken for our Sign of the Cross. Suddenly his hoofhand tacky and dothered.*)

ULLIN (*mortified*). Oh piglet. To crap on the Lord. Oh Master . . .

PAN. Some say this should be meat and drink to me . . . (*He hands back the child to his humiliated parents.*) Is that hunger?

ULLIN. Little pig'm allus hungry.

PAN. Feed him whether or not it is his hour. It is his Supper too.

ULLIN (*taking the baby to breast*). Little pig. To shite on the Lord.

PAN (*sensing*). Brother Gil?

GIL (*unhappy*). Master. Thou ask. We have a brother. Sir. Who say he shall not work. We say not work not eat. What must we do?

PAN (*sensing from them who this must be*). Vitus?

VITUS *bows his head in shame.*

Vitusbrother, if this be you, you put your bretheren to a deathly thing. Must they lay down like lambs before this wolf you choose to become? Meekly allow your ravening lay waste the fruit of their toil? Or blind you, starve you? till you work? Or drive you from them? Then you become a wolf to them in any case. Think. They must guard their food against you, night and day. The watchman by day no longer free to do his share of fruitful toil; nor the watchman by night, for he must sleep by day. You lay on two friends in living a burden of fruitless work, guarding against you; while the fruitful toil must be done, by two friends fewer. I call this deathly for it spells the beginning of the end of the world.

VITUS (*abased*). Lord . . .

PAN. I have something I must ask. We have a sister, misshapen from birth. I have heard her pray, for touch of my hand to set her poor back straight and true. Jehan.

*Trembling, she stands.*

Has any anything to say, why our sister's back should not be healed?

BROTHER IN WOOL. Master. Our sister were shapen crooked into this world. How can to set her straight be true?

JEHAN. For my ease, good friends . . .

SISTER AGNES (*not rhetorical; answers are sought*). Are we born to ease?

JEHAN. My fuller sharing in our work . . .

PAN. Work, work . . .

MOVINS. Master, work must be done.

SISTER MARTHA (*an older woman*). A back's a back. You are what you are. Stand straight in your heart. If man would stoop you, make it his task, uphill for him all the way; not yours to bow.

PAN. Cold comfort, Sister Martha.

SISTER MARTHA. Comfort is lies. Your crooked back's a sorrow, sets you aside. Make that your richness. A crooked torch may light dark corners where light of straight torch cannot go.

JEHAN (*weeping*). Gil, Brans and I have a bab in here. When it shall swell, weigh me a-down'ard, thrust un's head down to be born, I dread . . . my back may hinder somehow and the bab be harmed.

PAN. Sister Martha?

SISTER MARTHA. Well. But I do fear. Change her now, earth may somehow have her die when the child is born. Dark must strike somewhere.

JEHAN (*at last*). We need the child.

SISTER MARTHA (*at last*). Well . . .

OTHERS. Aymen. Aymen.

PAN *has* JEHAN *kneel before him. The others kneel also, hands joining in a circle with her, all eyes closed.*

PAN. Crooked sister, come away. Friends, bring her where I am. In darkness. Stillness. Before all time began.

I am alone. Before all light.

Now in me a thought: and I have eyes. I see around me, in the silent emptiness, Sun Moon, cold Earth and all the dust that are the stars.

I think, and I am free. I drift, down, down, toward this stone earth mantled in her water, turning, turning, half in darkness half in light. I think again. Things happen into being. Sisters and brothers of my thought, born of my will, and altogether free of me. In this forest, I mould a sister. Jehan.

What? Do I shape her badly? No. Time, stand. Earth, still. Waters, wait. Hand, steady. Jehan is not yet born. Her crookedness was all a dream she had before her birth. Her back is true. I shape her, ready. Brothers and sisters, breathe into her the breath of life.

*A gentle blowing from him, soon taken up by all: rising, falling, never broken, cold and inexorable as the dawn.*

Time, move. Earth, turn. Waters, flow. Jehan be born.

JEHAN *stirs, waking into a miraculous wholeness; to rise, erect, transfigured, and in tears of joy. From the others, shattered cries: 'Hallelujah!' 'Praise the Lord!'*

JEHAN *stands from now, in unbelieving ecstasy, unmoving.*

*The* BROTHER IN WOOL, *presumably a monk by day, begins singing to the old plainchant the hymn 'Oh come Oh come Emmanuel'. This gradually will be taken up; even by Heniot's clan, who do not know it, and who growl, a perfect fourth flat, in wild organum: rough, musicless, but never arbitrary — a primordial crescendo.* PAN *moves among his flock.*

PAN. Brother Movins. I smell from your skin, your flesh has lost its song.

MOVINS. Master we must work so hard.

PAN. Oh work's a riddle. Ask. 'This work I set my hands to, is this for better living? Need this be done?'

MOVINS. Master, well for Thee. I do have my toil. I'm pains this long time, with the bowing and the damp. I am ashamed. I am so dull a man. I feel my body is my death.

PAN. It is.

MOVINS. What song can my flesh sing now? My breath stink, hers stink, we'm neither to the other's tune no longer. If this be the way of our flesh, Thou may be Master of the Earth but cannot change that.

PAN. I have no answer. But it is your only life.

SISTER AGNES. He he. I'm a owl! (*Probably a respectable wife by day.*) He he! He he! I begin to fly! (*Is smearing her thighs and armpits with some strange green paste.*) White owl!

Flap flap! A-hu-hoo-oo, a-hu-hoo-oo! Flap clothy wings. Low across the town . . .! (*She lies prone on the ground, waving her arms slow, all flying in her head.*)

BRANS *lies on his back in joy, legs twining round* PAN's *forward thrusting shoulders as* PAN *caresses, fondles him.*

PAN. And you hate death? Brans brother, you hate death? Tell me you hate death.

BRANS. Filthy foul sow. Take from us. And us away. Stench, shite, filth, pain.

PAN. Yet she shall come.

BRANS. Well for Thou Sir. Whose spunk be cold.

PAN. Well for you whose spunk is warm. Shited into living, ripe with death. (*Head sad in melancholy labour:*) I am your rising and your life. I make myself a gift to you. Know your mirehood: to rise again and live.

BRANS (*torment*). Master. Thy stretching of me feel so black. Thy cock is crowned wi' thorns!

PAN. I harrow Hell? I vanquish Death? I make your sty parts glad?

BRANS. Ha a . . . I truly ride Thy broomstick now . . .

PAN. I brother you.

BRANS. My breasts! Milk from them! The milk from my breasts! The milk from my cock and my breasts . . .! Master . . .? (*Something is amiss . . .*) Ma- . . .?

PAN *pulls sharply away from him. Silence from all. They sense themselves surrounded.*

PAN. Quickly . . . Quickly . . . Quickly good people, away — !

*He is gone.*

ALL. Master . . .? (*Bewildered, bereft. A sudden flash. Beginning of screams. A shattering explosion.*)

*Smoke. Gradual flamelight. Moaning: amid trees heard burning, falling, bodies lie quivering, meat that had been people, rendered into heaps we cannot read.* MOVINS *uncomprehending, feeling at something alien lodged in his flesh.* ULLIN: *why her baby has no head? From the auditorium a slow branding hiss: black-silhouetted figures mount cautious with the elemental dread of space-travellers on a virgin planet: armoured*

*head to toe in gold, their visors' only orifice a square trap.
These creatures experience themselves as gold; the only holes
they acknowledge in their bodies are their mouths, for
utterance of the Truth vouchsafed to them alone. One bears
aloft a proud device, a branding-iron in shape of a dislocated
crucifix, hands and ankles swastified. It glows redhot, and
smoke from it; hissing.*

ARTAUD (*gentle*). Netsil. Netsil. Nerdlich thgin ni tsol. Ees su.
NoitPmeder ruoy. NoitAvlas ruoy. Eciojer.

*Witchcart; soldiers PEEK, PICKAVANCE heap indiscriminately
the living and the dead, bodies, pieces of bodies. One soldier
has a long-shafted shovel. At the cart stands MOTHER
MANUS, kindly nun-Artemis again, riven with redeemer's joy.*

PEEK (*quiet*). Lost on these Sir. These are primitives.

ARTAUD (*removes helmet of gold*). I grieve, for the pulp and
carrion of those whom our redemption has not come in time
to save. (*Takes up with joy the baby's head.*) Here's one at
least, was spared the tyranny of darkness! (*Riven with love
for the carnage around him.*) Rejoice! Rejoice! The Sons of
Truth are now the masters of the earth!

JEHAN. *Stunned, unharmed, she darts bewildered glances to
PEEK, PICKAVANCE, as wary they circle her, one with
shovel, the other with a mallet. In their irrational deep terror
they misread her every questioning gesture as an attempt to
launch at them some venomous sting. In mounting lather of
killneed, they utter inchoative strokes at her, never quite in
range, always to a brute guttural mindless roar. Suddenly the
one with the mallet sees his opening; and with a wild dumb
bellow leaps in to swing full ictus of it into the small of her
back. All recoil, dreading what prodigy she might from this
stroke become. She becomes nothing. Standing, stopped,
stooped, silent, agape and stupid, in mute unbelieving at the
damage of the stroke, her face the last we see. Darkness.*

# Part Two

*Hushed grave figures — ecclesiastic, secretarial, of early fifteenth century. Tribunal; chairs; a presiding throne. Documents. A stool, book, ink, quill. JUDGES severally conversing, one pondering a transcript. MOTHER MANUS, secular lady of the land, young middle-aged beauty tempered by station and grave duty. ARTAUD, monk again, all soldiering's stenchful necessity purged; another, JUNIOR JUDGE, younger, face and personality not clear to us yet. Chief of them PAPATRIX: grand-paternal; long white hair; concerned, kindly; but weary with this business. They take their places.*

*Up, slow, the prisoner shuffles, route well worn. Tight, shit-coloured convict-tunic; hair cropped, eyes staring, face ravaged, ankles hobbled, this figure not recognisable even for a woman, let alone the JEHAN she once was. Back buckled like a sow. An eternity, hobbled step by hobbled step, to reach her judges. Painfully she kneels amidst them. At book, quill poised, CLERK waits.*

MOTHER MANUS. Joan.

> When we first took you into care, you seemed very much to seek a positive relationship with us. You listened, searchingly, devouringly indeed, to everything we put to you. You showed a genuine need, to understand our meaning.
>
> After a while, you seemed not to want to hear us any more. You became unco-operative. Irresponsible. To all our questions, you gave carnival answers. As though you held us in contempt.
>
> You turned offensive. Hostile. Well. Adaptation is difficult. But for your own sake we had to subject you to considerable restraint.
>
> Now you are mute. You lapse. Into dumb, regressive apathy.
>
> What do you want us to do?

*No answer. CLERK notes this; scratching of quill.*

> We are going to try. This one last time. To see if we can make some contact with you Joan. You remember what these are. Our little tests.

*JUNIOR JUDGE holds book down for JEHAN to see: seem to be mediaeval woodcut illustrations. To JEHAN pictures are illegible.*

We haven't done these for a while. I know you find these tedious Joan. You would not if you co-operate. It is tedious for us too. But we have to track down what is causing you your difficulty Joan.

These pictures. You remember? And under each picture, five interpretations? We know you can't read the interpretations, we don't think worse of you for that, I'll read them for you. And you must tell me which interpretation you think is true.

Picture number one. A man lying down on his tummy. See? Now. What — Joan. Look at the picture Joan.

JEHAN *is staring at the* JUNIOR JUDGE: *he is a Brans, a lifetime self-repressed; an almost imperceptible twitch in him shows it.*

This man on his tummy. What would you say he is doing? Interpretation A? He is on vacation in the mountains? Do you think it is that? Joan? Or perhaps he is asleep by the sea. Or a soldier spying on the enemy. Or someone hiding because he has done something wrong . . .

PAPATRIX. Joan, how can we help you if you will afford no guidance? What you think this man is doing, don't be afraid to say. How could an answer get you into trouble?

ARTAUD. Joan. I don't believe — none of us believes — this is the true Joan offering us resistance. The Joan that Joan would be if Joan could only understand. That Joan is surely reaching to this helping arm that we extend. In hunger and thirst, aching to be one with us, in gladness and fulfilment. Wholeness. A Joan that shrinks from gladness, must be some sick Joan in you, other, dark, preventing you. Oh Joan your sickness is so deep, you cannot even feel yourself as sick. Help us to help you. Help us.

JUNIOR JUDGE (*with the book*). Jehan, this man . . .

JEHAN. Where is Gil? (*She looks at him.*) Where is Brans?

MOTHER MANUS. Joan —

JEHAN. Where is Vitus? Ullin? Little piglet? Movin, Greisel, Abb? I want go back my friends in living in the world! Work wi they! Play wi they! I want go back! I want — (*Silent.*)

PAPATRIX. Joan. You know that won't be possible. Where you lived was unhealthy. Here at least you are dry.

JUNIOR JUDGE (*easy, sure*). Here you are morally safe.

JEHAN. Can't shit in a bucket. Rim cut my arse. Sit wrong. My hole don't close up after, make me dirty. On bucket, hole won't open now. Shit beginnin not to come. You'm killin me! (*Snivelling.*)

PAPATRIX (*to* CLERK, *sotto*). Strike that.

MOTHER MANUS. We do not want you to be unhappy. How could we want that? It's because we want you happy that we bring you here. But truly happy. You may have thought you were happy in the forest. You were not. You see Joan —

JEHAN. Jehan. (*Silence.*) Jehan. (*Silence.*)

MOTHER MANUS. You see, Joan. In what you call the world, your forest, you thought you had no problem. But you did have. You were living in a — I would not call it a bad way but — Well, a — sick way. Joan. You were living in a sick way. You did not experience it as sick, how could you? That is why you want to go back. In the forest you could delude yourself you have no problem. It would be very nice if we could live in a forest and delude ourselves we have no problem. But we have to live in the real world Joan, reality; and it is a problem.

*Silence.*

PAPATRIX. The question is, in this case can such a transition be made? I am not hopeful.

*Silence.*

MOTHER MANUS. When you first came to us, we discussed what the seed of a man is for. You remember? To make a baby.

JEHAN. Seed of a man? Woman belly have the seed. Man milk it and it grow. (*Sudden:*) Bab cummin yurr. (*Bleak silence.*)

MOTHER MANUS. Very vernacular and charming Joan. Not good enough. I'm not saying those things you did with, your men, were wrong. I haven't the qualification in moral law. But that way of living does make for problems Joan. A man and a woman live together, in a little house, and make their babies, and they can shape the loves they have around each other. I'm not saying this way you will not encounter problems. But we are here to help you cope with these.

JUNIOR JUDGE. Of the things you did in the forest, which

would you now say was the most . . . most wicked? Those things with, hm, your men, or they with each other, in the night, that can't make babies? Or . . . Joan . . . To have abominable knowledge, of him you call your Master, Prince of Excrement. The Devil. Joan? Also, which seems most reprehensible to us, you burned a body of your dead. Beyond all hope of resurrection! Also the possessions. Burned. The waste.

JEHAN (*staring at him*). Where is Brans?

*Silence.*

PAPATRIX. Always this relapse.

*A silence, heavy.*

ARTAUD. Joan. Let us talk about pain. No one wants pain. Pain spoils our pleasure in our living. Oh, we think, if this were a world without pain . . . But think. What is pain? A message that our body sends us, from some sick part in us, eating our good life away. If that caused us no pain, how should we know it was there, to cut it out? It would grow in us, grow. And suddenly one day we die, because we had no warning. Pain is good. Sickness that sends no pain is deathliest of all.

MOTHER MANUS. Joan my child. Poor Brans had such a sickness. Not in his body. In what he thought about his body. A sickness in his thinking . . . How can we cut a blemish from the brain? One day perhaps we shall be able. I wish we could cut that sick part out of a suffering brain, like an eye from a potato Joan don't you?

JEHAN (*laugh*). We do cut eye out of spud yet spud with eyes we say be blind! (*She laughs.*)

MOTHER MANUS. Very apposite, Joan. (*Impressed.*) 'The potato is blind.' What if the potato told you it could see, because it had an eye? You have higher sight. You know better. Its eye is its blindness, so you cut it out.

JEHAN. Where are my men?

*Silence.* PAPATRIX *beckons her: kindly shows her a massive book full with entries.* JEHAN *is like a helpless needful child beside a kindly teacher.*

PAPATRIX. Joan. This, says Gil. This, says Brans. Beside Gil's name these words. Latin. Very important. Per adaptationem conformatus. That means Gil is better now. Brans. Relaxatus.

MOTHER MANUS. That is a very special word. Only we use it. It has very grave meaning Joan. The decision to relax a man. We yield him away. Must let him pass from our responsibility.

JEHAN. Let pass? Let Brans go?

PAPATRIX. To that, organ of the state . . . Not for our authority to oversee. Whose process it is, to discharge the more, unlovely functions, necessary to our wellbeing, as a, society of men.

JUNIOR JUDGE. He has had to be burned.

*The others are displeased at the nakedness of this.*

As must be done with all bad parts and rotten matter Joan. Or they spread sickness to us all.

JEHAN. Burned? Burn Brans' body? How were he dead? We burn Heniotbody, you say wrong! Brans dead? Brans not anywhere?

MOTHER MANUS. Joan that's the whole issue! He is not nowhere. He is in the lovely garden of the King.

JUNIOR JUDGE. The burning sees to that.

MOTHER MANUS. You have to understand. If Brans die sick, how can he be admitted to the lovely garden? We must burn his body before he die. For him to be clean. He is at peace now, in the garden above. So cleansed. He looks down upon you Joan. In pity, how you stray here. Stumble. He so yearns to reach his hand to you.

JEHAN. Burn? Brans? A living man? (*She begins to vomit.*)

ARTAUD (*torn for her*). The sickness masters her.

*All ward it off with crucifixes.* CLERK's *quill scratches.*

MOTHER MANUS. If death were the end. If our fire burned a man to nothing and for ever, where would be the sense in anything we do? We must be rational.

JEHAN. Lord! Master! Help me! Devils have me! Master! I be fallen among vampires! That have no arseholes and cast no shadow! Master! Help me! (*She thrashes, screaming. She spits at them, farts at them.*)

*The* JUDGES *are grave.* PAPATRIX *is unhappy, catching the eye of each. Mute wretched accord.* PAPATRIX' *own quill scratches.* JEHAN *looks in vain from one to another. None will meet her eye. Books are closed. Documents gathered. Brute soldiers* PEEK, PICKAVANCE *come.* JEHAN *searches face after face in bewilderment, terror. Tables, chairs, everything being removed: as though she exist no more.*

PAPATRIX. Brother Artaud. Since only the child can be saved, help her make ready.

ARTAUD *comes to* JEHAN, *his countenance a miracle of riven grief and love.*

ARTAUD. Oh Joan . . .

*Darkness on them as they go.*

*Night. Bleak moan of wind afar, like a human voice transformed. Shattered shuddering survivors of coven, one man,* ABB, *and one woman,* SISTER AGNES, *amid ruin of trees.* ENESTER *as* THE LORD: *Light of the World in ragged white, with guttering lamp and torn with thorns.*

THE LORD. We shall never be free. We are bound to the earth, bowed to the treadwheel of her seasons. The earth is slow. Our peril is, that that could turn our thinking slow; and our horizon narrow, to that drill of ground before us as we till and hoe. The horse is strong. The ass is obdurate. Yet both are fallen. Man piles the ass with burdens. The horse, he yokes to the plough and the mill, and flails to his mad fields of the shedding of blood. Surely the horse is dark in the head, never to reckon how stronger than the man he is; and the ass, dark, never to think to try his obduracy out, beyond the patience of a man. Man buys them both with shelter and food. Yet enter horse that stable, ass that stall, each dips his muzzle in the manger on man's terms; and his eternity of serfdom has begun.

Brother. Sister. We must think now. Must this be our destiny? For man is also our own enemy. He may have better ploughs than we, better tools for felling, sawing; to build what, where and how we never could, a comfort ease and beauty we could never. His skills may free him light as air, above such drudgery as weighs us downward. Yet I tell you, yet I tell you, for all that his advancement lighten him, always shall he fashion loftier drudgeries to mesh himself. It must run from some deep ill-sitting in his heart, this need for toil. As though for fear, in idleness, some well in him might open, and his dark water rise.

Upward ever, straining to breathe, he chokes. Upward, upward, ever building around himself, the unacknowledged tower of his own inalienable bondage to the soil. We knew how we are bowed. We knew how we are ripe with excrement and death. We found a time to play. We toiled, to live. He finds work for his time. He lives to toil. The skies above his world are red with burning.

SISTER AGNES. Why must the sick inherit the earth?

THE LORD. Sister Agnes. To seek to inherit the earth, itself is a sickness.

SISTER AGNES. How long must they rule?

THE LORD. I will not comfort you. Remember our sister Martha's words. Comfort is lies. Friends, truth is the staff through the valley of the shadow. The rising sun to come is black. Under it, we stand to be scattered, our gladness shredded and strewn to the wind, and all our health undone. They shall harness the dark waters of us all, to turn their mills of Satan. And the name of the earth shall be the Book of the Dead.

ABB. Master? What shall that make the King of Love? (*Shattered, trembling and alone.*)

THE LORD. What he always was. A hunted criminal.

SISTER AGNES. Master. I am afraid to die. I loathed the thought of death before. Now I am afraid. And such an execution . . .

THE LORD (*deathly*). I know.

The vampires promise beyond the flame a garden. I promise you nothing. Nothing. Long long long last obliterating agony, and no reward. Though in worlds we do not dream of yet, some might marvel how you could endure the flame; and wonder, Surely some great love sustained you? But these too have their flame to come. (*Bleak wind afar.*) We must go our ways. Sister Agnes far well. (*He kisses her forehead, making there the ancient sign.*)

SISTER AGNES. Master. Far well. Thank you for your love.

THE LORD. Brother Absalom (*Likewise.*) Far well.

ABB. Thank Thee. Master. Sister . . .

SISTER AGNES. Brother . . . (*Each lingers, then covert, severally goes.*)

THE LORD *remains. After a moment, he takes up something precious from the ground. The garb of Pan. He raises it high across his white arms to Heaven, hurling from west to east one long wild soundless howl of elemental grief. He sinks. Cold wind afar. Lovingly, with mystery and passion, he buries the Pan garb in the earth.*

THE LORD. Gently lay him, Saviour in His grave to sleep. The night could pass. A dawn could come. And sons and daughters of the morning; saying: 'We seek our Lord, and do not know where they have laid Him.' (*Last the head:*) Head of Heads, King of Kings, down, down, into the clay.

*Darkness.*

*The Passion of Joan.*

*Gentle sunlight. Song of birds.* JEHAN, *ugly in martyr's shift, grunting, almost at term, comes dragging a large torn branch to witchcart laden for her burning.* PEEK *and* PICKAVANCE, *crude soldiery, stand bored, sharing a covert cigarette.* JEHAN *pauses on her knees, back arched in back-labour posture: a contraction coming. A bleak staring toward the soldiers, but seeing nothing; self in this world no more.*

PICKAVANCE. Sergeant. Sergeant Peek.

PEEK. ?

PICKAVANCE. She wants a drag.

PEEK. Wha'?

PICKAVANCE *gestures toward* JEHAN *with his cigarette.*

Hey. Corporal. You give us that. After where her lips have been? She'll soon be smoking all she need.

*The contraction passes;* JEHAN *resumes painful dragging. She tries to heave the branch up onto the cart; cannot; pauses. Tries again. Cannot.* ARTAUD *comes, ravaged with pity for her; offers help.*

JEHAN. No. No Brother Artaud. What have light to do with darkness? Black eye must do it. (*She heaves, clambers up onto the cart, hauls. Another contraction.*)

ARTAUD. Oh Joan. I pray for you. That you won't feel too much.

JEHAN. Feel?

ARTAUD. Why witch, the flames.

JEHAN. Black eye must be cut out, to keep spud good.

ARTAUD. Oh Joan. Our toil for you was none of it in vain. I feel more gladness in you than in all were never lost. Can you . . . find in yourself, some little gladness?

JEHAN. Fast I can. I were a filth in the earth, among you — good folk . . . Now I burn to give you light.

ARTAUD. You chasten us all.

JEHAN. I know the flame shall hurt. I tried it a little. Wi'a lantern. (*She gulps.*) Brother Artaud. Do not weep . . . I leave earth clean! I found these. Grubbed they up for thee. Good brother. Bake they in my fire for thy good children. (*They are small early potatoes.* ARTAUD *uncertainly takes them.*)

PAPATRIX, JUDGES *silently gather;* MOTHER MANUS *of the trial scene, as* LADY ENESTER *now.* ENESTER: *ashen. All severely dressed. Birth is upon* JEHAN: *on her own stakewood, thrusting like a cow.*

LADY ENESTER. Not that way Joan. This way. This way. (*Righting her onto her back.* ARTAUD, ENESTER *offer shapeless assistance;* LADY ENESTER *will have none.*) Woman's business. —Push Joan. Push. No, a really hard push, Joan. (*The contraction passes.*)

ENESTER. I hate these occasions.

LADY ENESTER. Birth is messy.

ENESTER. Death. That we inflict.

LADY ENESTER. What alternative have we? At least she is not some poor astronomer persecuted by the forces of reaction, as in pagan times. Anaximander was it? for presuming to speculate on what took place above and below the earth?

ENESTER. Anaxágoras. And not astronomy so much. But proposing a myth, whereby the unexplained might yet be mapped. What else does any science do?

LADY ENESTER. At least we know the earth is flat. (*Contraction:*) A big push Joan. A really big one. Push with your bottom. As tho' you were — Hm. A really big push in your bottom Joan. (*The contraction passes.*)

ENESTER. What if Man all along were nothing but a cancer on the earth. Then all his progress were the cancer spreading.

*Contraction:*

LADY ENESTER. She's crowning! I can see his head!

*Quietly from nowhere,* EXECUTIONER *in hood; Soldiers with ugly tools for Jehan's burning —* PEEK *with three-hook dragging-iron,* PICKAVANCE *with rake. In chaos and ugliness the child is born, umbilicus bloodily cut, slimed homunculus hung up by the heels for* LADY ENESTER's *traumatic slap. Theatre fills with child's screaming.*

LADY ENESTER. A little son.

PAPATRIX (*discreet*). Daughter. Daughter.

LADY ENESTER. A lovely little son. Clean him.

*She thrusts the child into the arms of* ARTAUD. *Nauseated by mucus and slime, he stumbles away.*

Quickly.

JEHAN *is already crawling clumsily up onto the wood. Movement, soldiers;* LADY ENESTER *washing her hands.*

That bird singing.

ENESTER. Songthrush. Turdus philomelus.

LADY ENESTER. Species subspecies subsubspecies. Turdus turdus, turdus simplex, turdus complex. Oh this fissiparous chaos of unrationalised nature. One aberrancy has only to take and a whole new class.

'JOAN' *stands fixed, as though hoops clamp her: at breast, waist, and knees. No wood, no stake. Solemn around her:* JUDGES, PAPATRIX, SOLDIERS, CLERK, LADY ENESTER, ENESTER. *From the town a* MR *and* MRS VITUS *with their child have come. A* SISTER AGNES, *covert, watches.* ENESTER's *face is a mask. Unhappily he gives the nod to have it over.*

*A sound of sudden flame. No simulation; rather, moral presence of* JEHAN's *dying. Her struggling body, thrusting Adam-apple, working face and starting eyes, sear into us her agony. Roar of encroaching storm of flame, annihilative force: inly she nearer, nearer to that threshold beyond which only darkness. She twists her face to one then another of us, to rivet into us the meaning of her extermination as a living soul.*

*Now she sees* ENESTER. *Crazed in her pain she recognises him. Struggles to reach him, her dry racked voice be heard of him. As though top hoop sundered, her body slumps forward, arm toward him pointing:*

JEHAN. Jesu . . .!

ENESTER'*s face is a mask. Stupid* PICKAVANCE *begins to grizzle:*

PICKAVANCE. We'm burnin a saint! We'm burnin a saint! (*He snaps the rake-shaft, fashions a crude cross, to hold it clumsily between her and her vision. The heat forces him back.*

'JOAN' *spills towards us. What light there was goes out. Soon all is as it was. Gentle dappled shadows; song of birds.*

JUDGES *etc. uneasily shift.* MR *and* MRS VITUS *and the child go home.* SISTER AGNES *moves ashen away.*

LADY ENESTER. Husband? When she cried to Jesus, why should she look at you?

ENESTER. Who knows what she saw? I've not a notion.

*They go.*

PEEK, PICKAVANCE *drag, rake, heap the smoking char. Pulverise it. Smuts that escape, they stamp on, stamp on. Nothing, nothing of the contamination must remain. They sweep, pound all to nothing. Last they hose all immaculately clean. There is no Jehan in the world.*

*Night. Bleak wind, forward, disturbed. A filthy shape, subhuman, thrusts obscenely between forks of a branch he pins to the ground, kissing, biting, ravaging. Once this was* GIL. *Once this was the birthstump near.*

GIL. Sky red. Another farm afire. 'Aa! Help, water, help! Our farm's afire, Black Giles have been!' (*He utters mock cries of cattle, horses, poultry in distress.*) Ay lad. An left thy mother an thy sisters weepin. 'Where is our little son? Our little brother?' Sniff an smell for his buggered sty me ladies, here he be. Down, lad. Down, farmson, down! Under! Black Giles ravage thy father's farm, now thee. Sty lad. Sty. Sty. Sty! (*Thrusts with lust into the struggling branch.*)

No. I shall ave thee be a dukeson. Whiteflesh, scented, Bibled, schooled. I'll master thee. Heir to thy father's lands be thou? I'll ground thee. Spike thee ream thee spit thee split thee. Ur. Ur. For all thy lute an Latin my come'll sully thee. A. A . . . Now I'll break thee for thy filthiness. Joint thee. Eat thee. (*Splits, snaps, gnaws at struggling branch. Eases.*)

I shall thrust my head in the earth. Shit up in the sky, papapapapa! Into the bellies o birds on the wing. Squawk plummet flap an flutter, fowls to earth all busted and awry. Thb thb thb thb. I shall plait me a crown from their feathers, reddle my face wi their blood, wipe my arse and stand so mighty, such a fierce lord, men shall call me king. King Giles, whose shit shall be death to things living.

I shall hire myself. To do man's shittin for him. Leave him free for loftier matters. While I shall lumber in the thickets, full to bustin wi the shit o the world. The tips of it, out through my mouth, nostrils, earholes, eyes. Men shall love me for the Beast of Time.

They shall enthrone me judge. They'll bring me their children for my daily food. I'll gorge, such a size, heads bones and arms of children champed, chawed, banked and tamped thick down inside my stretching gut. On judgment day I shall thrust up the mountains of my arse, and vent to the ends of the earth the thunder of my silage. The shards of my dung shall lay waste the cities of men, the burdens of my ordure lay their houses waste, and in their air bequeathe them such a foulness, none shall live. None, I say. None. And then, when I am God, I'll straddle the sky, part my hatch above the earth, and in one slow wet voiding merd it all. (*Eases. Wind bleak, receding.*)

Poor Gil. Poor arse. Poor little cock. Poor deathly man. Poor Gil. They say I am sick of a Ramsbury fever. Yet I had a daughter. Born. Jehan Brans I. Long time gone. (*Maudlin, he rocks the branch in his arms.*) Lullay. Sleep. Thy mother's burned. Thy other father's burned. She for a witch. He, trussed wi his likes on the ground and set afire, faggots for witches to be burned. Daughter hush. Thou have one father yet. He'll bring thee through the dark wood safe. (*Strange imagined cry of hers, ever on the one same falling semitone:*) 'Faither . . . Faither . . .' Hush daughter. Easy. Thy father bring thee home.

*He looks round him at birthstump: some dim memory.*

How be such ashes here? Charnel. What monster ave tore these white lambs' throats? 'Faither . . . Faither . . .' Quick hurry home. Werewolf was here last night. We're next in his path. Home, house, in, hurry. Shut door behind us, bolt it. In now. In. Home. Safe.

'Faither . . . Faither . . .' Smell him. Werewolf. Hereabout. Twilight, his hour. He sniff around the house outside. Almost feel him. He nuzzle the foot of our door. No, daughter, easy. We're in, he's out, lie in thy cradle.

Smell him. Near. Near too near. With us. In. (*Own breath becoming raucous, hands more clawlike.*) Wolfstink. Wolfstep. Indoors wi us all along. Waited for night. 'Faither . . .' Father shall guard thee. Cover thee against him, my own body. Husha. Husha! Little lamb I love thee! (*He sinks his teeth into the branch. Eases, unwolved again. One last pale flicker of a man.*) In the morning, what he woke and saw . . .

*Wind curls away to silence.*

I had a daughter. Where is she? Ee-ee. Dawnlight. Burn me. Day burn my eye! (*He staggers in pain.*) Aa! Yellow flower open . . . Blind me . . . (*He sinks, covering his eyes; a high thin almost voiceless whine of pain. Silence.*) I can't see. (*He suddenly turns on us:*) I can't see!

*Cut.*


### The Triumph of Death

*The throbbing of the bell: receding now.* PEEK, *in institutional white, works almost inaudibly at an abacus, making entries into a miniature book.* PICKAVANCE *likewise, kneels bulling at one spot of the floor throughout, with the tip of one finger. Foreground: gross figure squatted excretorally on tripos-stool in sixteenth century doctoral black — the* LUTHER *of the Cranach portrait, with* ULLIN's *face.*

LUTHER. Gentlemen of Wittenberg. Daily I labour. On this
    monastery privy. Postern tower in the city wall.
    My perineum stretched. My rectum seized. A giant on his
    wrangling-stool, brought low. My mother was Joan of Arc.

My father was Gilles de Rais. Of which of us can something similar not be said? My name is Luther. Brother Martin. My bowel won't shift. My head can comprehend the world. My sphincter will not part. My posture as Man is mortified.

*Zzz. Zzzz. (Traces fly around 'his' head then 'his' rear.)* Musca vomitoria. Waiting in hopes. He knows his element.

In the beginning. A beast of the earth. Eyes to the ground, his mirror the soil. One day experimentally lifts up his paws. Trusts his weight to his hindlegs only. Stands. Head raised; nostrils sniffing a new sweet air — all of three feet above his fellowapes' excretal odours. He looks up. New mirror: the sky. New proud notion of his biped self, reflected there. God. Who else? A Father in Heaven.

Wait. What's this? Soft, slithering out behind. Ape turns. Looks down. The brown snake steams. Ape wrinkles his nose. Ape is uneasy. New Father in Heaven must not see this. Our apex of the ape is not with this. Did not do this. Voice from Heaven. Head. *(Deathly:)* Awareness. Ape shits, and knows it. Ape fucks; now knows it. And now ape knows he'll die. His Eden's lost; and ape is Man.

*Zzz. Zzz. (Fly goes under 'his' skirts.)*

There's the serpent in the garden. Brown, moist, glistening in the grass. Ba'al Zebul. Lord of Flies. How shall image of that be wiped, from the mirror in the sky? The merd of that, in this original garden, be redeemed?

Daily I travail in this tower. Martyr to Man. My face strains up to the deathless chastity of Heaven. My old nick arsehole strains over his sulphurous pit. My head and sty perforce are yoked. Oh for a garden again, in which no shitting and no fucking and no dying. Oh for a transcendent life above, where we shall soil not, neither shall we sperm, not yet decay.

The light of it flashed on me. The road to such a yonderland lies only through death of this life. What else is Adam's evolution? Unease to shame. Shame to guilt. Guilt into debt. Debt to mortgage. Ever, ever to be 'redeemed'. Ever, ever, and never, to be 'worked off'. By work be justified? Making our good pile? By honest out-put? Our sublime Gross Product, secular popes exhort us to? Our excrement transmute, to the acceptable faeces of Gold? Sick alchemy. All for Be'elzebub.

All for our flight from the sty. This world we build, to justify and save us, is a delirium: of our fecality itself. A construct from shit. I see it clear. God was our wholeness all along. Our fracture is our fall. This world is an antic of the Devil. Stercor, made head. There is no garden above. The prayer is vain, and blasphemy. To quench this life, that we are given and have, for a yonder life that we shall never: what else is that but Satan's victory?

Get thee behind me, world. No such redeeming's needed. I'll shit when I am able. I'll fuck where I am welcome. I'll die when I must. My shitting and my fucking and my dying come from God. Here is my garden. Here I'll play. I'll trust my Maker, and I'll live. The Resurrection of the Body is in this life.

It is my moment of illumination in the tower. My bowel moves. I see Father in Heaven, Pope on earth, Emperor, Judge, Usurer, turn to skeleton and dust. My rectum relaxes. My sphincter crowns, and opens. Remission is upon me. And all the centuries of banked pathology that we call History come down to be undone.

*Is motionless. Silence. Click of abacus.* PICKAVANCE *bulls quietly away.*

MOTHER MANUS *is here, our modern incarnation of the alchemical Virgin of the Tarot: hair a blond meringue, face a gleaming fard of blush cosmetic, aglow with the lethal lustre steroids bring. She seems a doctor.*

LUTHER. Zzz. Zzz. (*This time inwardly seizes at proximity of fly.*)

For all which I am in the madhouse still. My shitting was your pass to salvation, now it's sold. The Devil's dead, you say. Old hat. Behind you. Say that, and he smiles. Devil's an old nick- name, for our compulsion to death. The past is another country. The past is not another country. There is no escape from history.

MOTHER MANUS. I think we've heard enough of, defecation. Do you not?

*Sudden click click of abacus from* PEEK, *entries in book.*

And of copulation.

*Stricken silence from both* PEEK *and* PICKAVANCE.

And, of . . . hm, the third matter.

*From* PEEK *and* PICKAVANCE *a panicked click click, rub rub.*

Brother Martin? (*From* LUTHER *nothing.*) Really your obsession is a blemish. (*From* LUTHER *nothing.*) You are not balanced.

LUTHER. No.

MOTHER MANUS. Really you must try to be more balanced. (*From* LUTHER *nothing.*) How are the pains in our back?

LUTHER. Worse.

MOTHER MANUS. What do we think causes the pains?

LUTHER. The substances going through my walls.

MOTHER MANUS. Which substances?

LUTHER. I have to supply the world with golden butter. Mine is the out-put of exclusively sweet butter. I myself of course have no more butter content than a fly would leave. Hm hm. That is starvation. But it's worth it. I am Noah's Ark. The boat of salvation and respect. Zzz. Zzz. (*Swat.*) The butter comes out of me almost white. It is obviously a sugarcone. You would be surprised how many distinguished citizens live on its slope.

MOTHER MANUS. Not at all. Most people are living on that slope now. This is the twentieth century.

LUTHER (*Blinks. At us. As though dimly perceiving us, then abandoning the effort.*) Have you heard any more about the banknotes?

MOTHER MANUS. Why?

LUTHER. I belong to the banknotes.

MOTHER MANUS *waits.*

It's a just system. My breath cannot come out of me anywhere. I am the stove for the state. I legislate the bankdrafts. No ventilation. Only breathe out through speakingtubes. Suffocation. Perish of death. All the same: silence is golden.

*Swat. Looks around her. Click, rub.*

I am a banknote factory seven floors high. Seven white floors. C major. Discord really is a crime. This white mill from above

is credible. But below. The stretchings. The terrible stretchings.
It's the food. Continually stretching me. Awful system. But I
am the monopoly. The paragon of suffering. The apex of
pure product. Zzz. Zzz.

MOTHER MANUS. You think it just that you should suffer?

LUTHER. I am the most abominable meaning of the world.
Abominable that a world like this should come to light. This
white house seven storeys high. Established on soil.

But I shall be whited in abundance, purest white.

Yes.

MOTHER MANUS (*at last*). Head. (*From* LUTHER *nothing*.)
Head.

LUTHER. Yes, irreplaceable.

MOTHER MANUS. Father.

LUTHER. Yes, mother.

MOTHER MANUS. Hair.

LUTHER. Hat, hat.

MOTHER MANUS. Paper.

LUTHER. Official. Official paper. White. I am polytechnic
irreplaceable. As owner of the world I am but did not cause
this madhouse.

MOTHER MANUS. Snake. Serpent. Snake.

LUTHER (*after thought*). I like paralysis best.

MOTHER MANUS (*at last*). Heart.

LUTHER. Yes, mind. Mind. Irreplaceable. Station for station
must keep their proper governmental place. So nothing be
hide behind. So nothing be behind. Nothing behind. Nothing.

*Click. Rub.*

MOTHER MANUS. Swim.

LUTHER. Drown. Once I almost drowned.

*Swat! Swat!*

MOTHER MANUS. Moon.

LUTHER. Sun. Sun.

MOTHER MANUS. Stars.

LUTHER. Fixed.

MOTHER MANUS. Caress. Caress.

LUTHER. A word one cannot write very well. I write it singular and it is cares.

MOTHER MANUS. Love.

LUTHER. Great abuses of the person.

MOTHER MANUS (*at last*). World.

LUTHER (*at last*). Owner. I am triple owner of the world. I am the Triply Imperial One. I am these titles too. Owners of the world are subject to extraordinary torment. Like a statue. I legalise a gold hem round my skirt. But the lazy remain ill.

MOTHER MANUS. How 'ill'?

LUTHER. Dirty I mean poor. I mean poor. The lazy remain poor. I am universal since the death of God.

MOTHER MANUS. Who is God?

LUTHER. My father. I came out of his mouth. Ugh. Say no more. Silence is golden.

MOTHER MANUS (*at last*). How do you mean, you are 'universal'?

LUTHER (*after thought*). Yes. Universal is . . . increment. Capital is the sublime conclusion.

MOTHER MANUS (*at last*). Good.

*Silence.*

I'm glad.

*Silence.* LUTHER *lays head in her lap, eyes unblinking out at us.*

Heaven. Hell. All that antique delirium. We're humanists now. We've got it right.

*She fixes on us a friendly smile; that stays fixed, a rictus of the skull. Click. Rub. Silence. Out.*